Pony-Crazed Princess

Princess Ellie's Mystery

Read all the adventures of Princess Ellie!

#1 Princess Ellie to the Rescue
#2 Princess Ellie's Secret
#3 Princess Ellie's Mystery

Pony-Crazed Princess

Princess Ellie's Mystery

by Diana Kimpton

Illustrated by Lizzie Finlay

Hyperion Paperbacks for Children

New York

For Liam

First published in the United Kingdom in 2004 as
The Pony-Mad Princess: A Puzzle for Princess Ellie
by Usborne Publishing Ltd.
Based on an original concept by Anne Finnis

For information address
Hyperion Paperbacks for Children, 114 Fifth Avenue,
New York, New York 10011-5690.

Printed in the United States of America

First U.S. edition, 2006

3 5 7 9 10 8 6 4 2

This book is set in 14.5 point Nadine Normal.

ISBN-13: 978-0-7868-4872-0
ISBN-10: 0-7868-4872-3

Visit www.hyperionbooksforchildren.com

Chapter 1

"Let's explore," said Princess Ellie. She stopped Rainbow at the entrance to the woods near the palace. The path through the woods was a long, dark tunnel. On one side was a high brick wall. On the other, trees grew so close together that their branches arched overhead and shut out the sun.

"Are you sure?" said her best friend, Kate. Moonbeam, the palomino she was riding,

fidgeted anxiously, her golden coat gleaming in the sunshine. The palomino was the most nervous of Ellie's four ponies.

"Yes," said Ellie, firmly. She wasn't ready to go back to the palace yet. When she was there, she had to be Aurelia, not Ellie. She had to follow rules and behave like a real princess. Out here, she was free to do as she liked.

Ellie squeezed with her legs, and Rainbow stepped forward obediently, her ears pricked. Kate followed close behind on Moonbeam.

"It's spooky in here," said Kate nervously, as they rode into the shade of the trees.

"Don't be silly," laughed Ellie. "You don't believe in

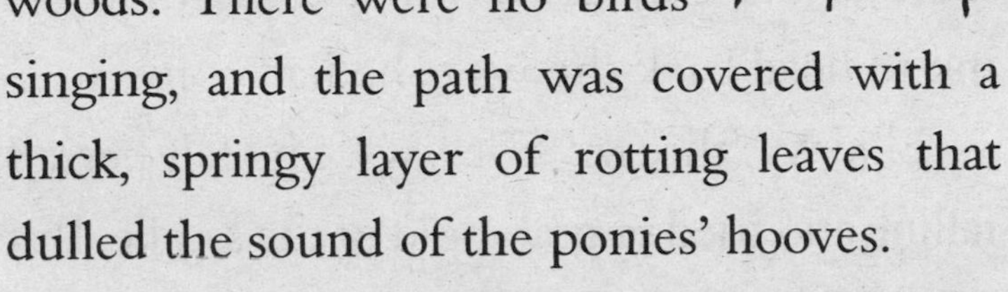

ghosts, do you?" Riding Rainbow gave her confidence. The gray pony was brave and reliable.

It was very quiet in the woods. There were no birds singing, and the path was covered with a thick, springy layer of rotting leaves that dulled the sound of the ponies' hooves.

As they rode deeper and deeper into the forest, Ellie looked around at the moss-covered wall and the damp tree trunks.

Kate's right, she thought. *It is kind of spooky in here.*

She pushed the gray pony into a trot, eager to reach the sunshine on the other side as quickly as possible.

Rainbow seemed uneasy, too. She tucked

her head and nickered nervously.

Suddenly, Rainbow stopped. Ellie was taken completely by surprise, and she shot forward out of the saddle. Rainbow didn't give Ellie time to recover her balance. Instead, the gray pony whirled around, trying to head back the way she had come.

Ellie was thrown sideways. She felt herself falling and tried to grab hold of the saddle. But she had already gone too far. With a loud thud, she landed flat on her back on the ground, clutching the reins tightly in one hand.

"Are you all right?" asked Kate, trotting over on Moonbeam.

Ellie wasn't sure. She lay motionless for a moment, shocked by the force of her landing. Then she cautiously moved her arms and legs a little. To her relief, there was no pain. Nothing was broken. Only her pride was damaged. "I think so," Ellie finally replied, as she climbed slowly to her feet. She brushed the dirt from her pale pink jodhpurs and straightened the pink-and-gold-silk cover on her helmet.

Kate looked relieved. "I think Rainbow would be back at the stable by now if you hadn't kept hold of the reins."

"Easy, girl," said Ellie gently, as she walked up to the tense, uneasy pony. She reached out and stroked her neck. "There's nothing to be scared of."

Rainbow relaxed at the sound of Ellie's voice and rubbed her head gently on Ellie's shoulder, taking comfort in her soothing touch.

"Should we go back?" asked Kate. "We don't want another accident."

"No," said Ellie. "I think Rainbow's all right now. Plus, all my books say you should never let a pony win." She put her foot in the stirrup and mounted quickly. As soon as Rainbow felt Ellie's weight in the saddle, the pony started trying again to head back the way they had all come.

"It's not time to go home yet," Ellie said firmly. She turned the pony around, to face the spot where she had just been spooked. This time, Ellie was prepared.

Rainbow walked forward reluctantly, glancing from side to side and snorting nervously. Then, at exactly the same place as before, she suddenly stopped again.

This time Ellie didn't lose her balance. But she was still shaken. What was wrong with Rainbow? She had never acted like that before. "Go on, girl," Ellie said encouragingly, as she pushed the pony on with her legs. Her voice sounded extra loud in the stillness of the woods.

But Rainbow didn't go forward. Instead, she whirled to the left. Ellie hadn't been quick enough to stop her, so she made Rainbow keep turning until the pony was again facing the spot where she had started. Then Ellie tried to make her walk on.

Rainbow took a step backward, then whirled suddenly to the right. Ellie's heart was pounding as she struggled to stay in the saddle.

"I'll try going in front," said Kate. "Maybe Rainbow will follow us." But Moonbeam refused to go past the gray mare. She just stood still and wouldn't move.

"What's wrong with them?" Ellie asked. "There's nothing there."

"Nothing we can *see*, anyway," said Kate.

Ellie felt a thrill of excitement mixed with fear. "I just remembered something," she said. "Some people believe horses can see ghosts."

Kate looked around nervously. "I told you these woods were spooky."

Ellie peered down the shadowy path ahead. Was there really something there—something only Rainbow could see?

Chapter 2

"Are you going to try again?" asked Kate.

"I don't know," said Ellie. "What if there *is* something there . . ." Her voice trailed off. Was she being silly? Was she worrying about nothing?

Kate glanced at her watch. "Well, we should probably be getting back," she said hopefully. "My grandmother will be angry if I'm late."

"No, she won't," laughed Ellie. Kate's grandmother was the palace cook, and she never seemed to get angry. "But my parents will be." For once Ellie was pleased that the King and Queen were so strict about mealtimes. It gave her and Kate the perfect excuse to leave those spooky woods.

The two girls turned their ponies and headed back. It was a relief to ride out into the sunshine. After one last glance back at the dark woods, they cantered home to the palace.

By the time they were back at the stable, Ellie felt much calmer. From a safe distance, the idea of haunted woods once again seemed more exciting than frightening. "Do you think it really was a ghost?" she asked Kate, as they filled the ponies' water buckets.

"It must have been," Kate replied. "It's the only explanation I can think of."

Ellie bit her lip thoughtfully as she moved the hose from a full bucket to an empty one. "But I thought ghosts prowled corridors and slid through walls. What would a ghost be doing in the woods?"

Kate laughed. "Maybe one of your ancestors liked growing trees." She waved her hands above her head and started running toward Ellie. In a spooky voice she said, "Ooooh! I'm Archduke Edgar, the ghostly gardener. And I'm coming to get you!"

As Kate came toward her, Ellie sprayed her with the hose. Kate squealed, grabbed the hose, and sprayed back.

The water fight lasted until it was broken up by Meg, the palace groom. By then, both girls were dripping wet and giggling.

"I don't know what's got into you two today," said Meg. "You'd better go home and dry off."

Ellie ran up the stairs to her very pink bedroom (the King's idea) with pony posters on the walls (her idea). She couldn't stop thinking about the woods. Was there really a ghostly gardener, or could there be something even more frightening out there? It was a real mystery, and Ellie was determined to solve it. She decided to start by asking her governess. Miss Stringle had a passion for royal history. She was sure to know whether anything weird had ever happened in those woods.

With her plan in mind, Ellie bounced into the schoolroom the next morning full of enthusiasm. Her heart sank, however, as she saw the selection of strangely shaped spoons laid out on Miss Stringle's desk.

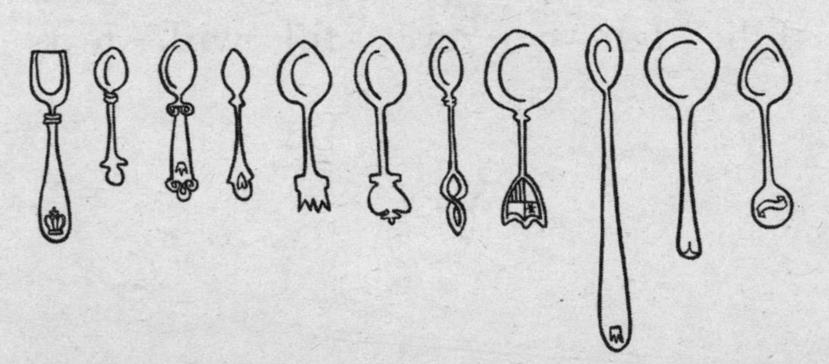

It was a test on table manners, and she had completely forgotten to study.

The soup spoon was easy to identify.

So was the extra-long one, because she used that one so often for ice-cream sundaes. The other spoons had her completely stumped.

"No, no, no," said Miss Stringle in exasperation, as Ellie made yet another wild guess. "Please try to concentrate, Princess Aurelia."

Ellie cringed. She hated her real name almost as much as she hated the test.

Miss Stringle waved the source of Ellie's latest mistake in the air. "This spoon is not for pickled onions. It is *only* for eating caviar in coddled eggs."

Ellie felt her eyes fill with tears.

Concentrating wouldn't have made any difference. She didn't know the answers. She wished all the spoons would just disappear in a puff of smoke.

They didn't. Instead, the schoolroom door burst open, and in swept the King and Queen. They both looked a little flustered.

Miss Stringle curtsied deeply. "Is there anything wrong, Your Majesties?"

"The Emperor and Empress of Andirovia are arriving this afternoon on a state visit," said the Queen.

"I know," said Ellie. The whole palace had been in turmoil for days. An army of servants had scrubbed and cleaned in preparation for the great event.

"But we've only just found out that they're bringing their son," continued the

Queen, a nervous edge in her voice.

"Prince John's the same age as you," said the King. "And he's sure to be bored while we conduct our official business with his parents. So we've decided you must entertain him for the whole week."

"It will be fun for you to have a friend," added the Queen.

"I already have a friend," said Ellie, firmly. She wasn't sure she wanted another one, especially a boy.

"But Kate's not a princess," said Miss Stringle. "It would be so much better for you to have a royal friend."

Ellie glared at her. She hated to hear Kate criticized just because her grandmother was a cook instead of a queen.

"Of course, you won't be able to have

your lessons while he's here," said the King, with a smile.

Ellie felt better immediately. A whole week with no school would be nice. It would be worth putting up with having a boy around if it meant not having to do homework. "Does that mean I can stop now?" she asked, with what she hoped would be a last glance at the dreaded spoons.

The Queen laughed. "Of course, you can, Aurelia. That way, you will have plenty of time for one last ride." As she turned to leave, she added, "Our visitors are arriving at five. Please wear your ermine."

Ellie stared at her mother in disbelief. "What do you mean—last ride?" she asked.

"It should be obvious," said the Queen.

"It's your duty to keep Prince John

happy," explained the King. "That will take all your time, so, while he is here, there is to be absolutely no riding, no playing with ponies, and no sneaking off to spend time at the stable."

Without another word, the King and Queen turned and walked out of the room.

Chapter 3

Ellie was horrified, but she knew there was no point in arguing. Once her parents started talking about duty, she could never change their minds. Duty was the downside of being a princess. So was wearing pink, having waving lessons, and taking tests about spoons. The upside was having four ponies.

She spent the rest of the day with her ponies, filling her mind with sights and smells to carry her through the ponyless week ahead. First, she took Shadow, the Shetland, and went for a drive through the deer park in the carriage. Then, Meg gave Ellie a jumping lesson on Sundance, and, after lunch, Ellie explored the banks of the stream on Moonbeam. She was so busy that she forgot all about the incident in the woods.

The hours went by too quickly—much faster than they would have in school. Before Ellie had a chance to ride Rainbow, it was time for her to get ready to welcome the royal visitors. She walked slowly through the stable, giving each pony a last pat and promising to be back as soon as she could. Then she reluctantly returned to the palace.

The royal hairdresser was waiting for

Ellie in her room when she got back. He tugged at her unruly curls with a comb as she sat on a pink velvet chair staring sadly into the pink-edged mirror.

"Oh, my," said the hairdresser, wrinkling his nose in disgust. He pulled a piece of straw from her hair and held it out at arm's length as if it might bite. "What has Your Royal Highness been doing?" he asked.

"Having fun," replied Ellie, miserably. She didn't feel like talking. She already missed her ponies, and it was only a few minutes since she had last seen them.

An hour later, Ellie met her parents at the main entrance to the palace. She was cleaner, but not happier. Her curls had been pulled and pushed into ringlets and tied with pink bows. The silver sandals on her feet were trimmed with crystal beads, and her long pink velvet dress was trimmed with ermine around the hem of its full skirt. The ermine, however, was fake. Even duty couldn't persuade Ellie to wear fur from dead animals.

"You look beautiful, Aurelia," said the Queen as she straightened the tiara on Ellie's head. The Queen was wearing her own best crown, and she was dripping with diamonds.

The King peered toward the palace gates. "They're coming," he announced. "I can see their car." He tugged at the jacket of his royal suit to make sure it was still straight, and adjusted the angle of his ceremonial hat.

Ellie followed her parents down the wide stone steps as a limousine swept up to the entrance and pulled to a halt in front of them. A footman opened the rear door, and out stepped the royal visitors.

The Emperor came first, dressed in a naval uniform decorated with an impressive number of medals. Ellie immediately wondered if he was as fierce as he looked. The beard that covered the bottom half of his face made it hard to see if he was smiling.

The Empress looked much friendlier. She smiled warmly at Ellie. "You must be Princess Aurelia," the Empress said, as she kissed her lightly on the nose. Ellie was surprised, but tried not to show it. She assumed that this was some strange Andirovian custom.

"And this is our son, Prince John," growled the Emperor. He pushed forward a boy who was wearing a uniform identical to the one he wore, but with no medals.

Ellie hesitated for a moment, wondering if she should kiss Prince John's nose or shake his hand. She didn't feel like doing either. She wished he hadn't come.

Her mother nudged her and whispered firmly, "Say hello, Aurelia."

Ellie forced herself to smile, and held out her hand. "I'm delighted to meet you," she lied.

Prince John took her hand limply and gave it an unenthusiastic shake. "I'm really pleased to be here," he said, but he clearly didn't mean what he said, either.

"I'm sure you'll have a lot of fun together," said the Queen as she led them all to the banquet hall.

Ellie doubted it. She didn't like the look of Prince John at all. How was she going to survive a whole week with such a sulky, miserable boy and no ponies?

Chapter 4

The Queen took the Emperor's arm as they walked into the banquet hall. The King followed with the Empress, leaving Ellie to accompany Prince John. Luckily, there was no need to make polite conversation—the fanfare of trumpets was so loud that it was impossible to talk.

The banquet hall glittered with crystal and silver. The other guests were already assembled, so the meal began as soon as the two royal families were settled in their seats. To Ellie's disappointment, hers was next to Prince John's. She'd have to think of something to talk about.

"Did you enjoy your journey?" she asked, politely.

"No," snapped the prince. "I was seasick."

"But you came by car."

Prince John looked at her as if she were the stupidest person in the world. "Before we were in the car, we were on a ship," he explained. "I'm always sick on ships."

"Oh," said Ellie, wondering what to say next. A discussion of being sick didn't seem like a good idea for dinner conversation. Fortunately, the food arrived at that point, and for once, Ellie was pleased that Miss Stringle had taught her not to speak with her mouth full. By eating very slowly and taking several extra helpings, she managed to keep it full for most of the meal.

To her relief, Prince John left the table as soon as he had finished his strawberry pie. "I should go to bed," he said. "It's been such a long day."

"Of course, dear," said the Empress, from across the table. "You must be exhausted. You may go on up to bed."

Ellie suspected that Prince John just wanted to miss the boring speeches, but she didn't argue. She was far too happy seeing him go. She no longer had to find ways to make polite conversation with him.

Unfortunately, there was no such escape the next morning. Prince John was in the sunroom waiting for Ellie when she came downstairs. He no longer wore his uniform and naval hat. Instead, he wore a shirt and tie and his everyday crown. But he still looked as bored as he had the night before.

"What would you like to do today?" Ellie asked.

"What do you suggest?" Prince John replied with a shrug. He ran his finger around the inside of his shirt collar, trying to pull it away from his neck.

For the first time, Ellie felt a twinge of sympathy for him. He looked as uncomfortable in his clothes as she felt in her stiff white blouse and tartan skirt. Maybe, like her, he'd have preferred to be wearing jeans and a T-shirt.

"There's chess," Ellie suggested.

"That's boring," the prince sneered.

"Or hangman?"

"Too childish."

"How about snakes and ladders?" said Ellie, impatiently. Her sympathy was quickly vanishing.

Prince John waved his hand toward the window. "Can't we do something outside?" he asked.

Ellie immediately thought of riding. But she reluctantly pushed the idea away and suggested croquet instead.

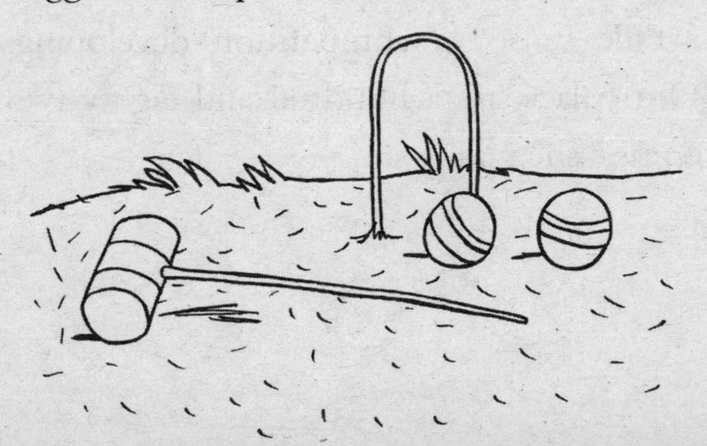

The prince agreed without enthusiasm.

He seemed even more annoyed when they started playing. Ellie knew knocking balls through hoops wasn't the most exciting activity in the world, but she had never before met anyone who seemed so bored by it. Halfway through the game, he stopped playing and started staring at the surrounding countryside instead.

Desperate for something to talk about, Ellie tried telling him more about the palace. "We have a lovely stream through the grounds," she said.

"We have a river through ours," said the prince.

Ellie sensed a competition developing. "Our palace has a hundred and eighty-two rooms," she said.

"Ours has four hundred and fifty," Prince John immediately replied.

"We have our own private beach," said Ellie, firmly. She was sure he couldn't beat that.

"Only one?" replied Prince John in a mocking voice. "We have five miles of private coastline and our own marina."

Ellie's mind raced. There must be something in her kingdom that was better than what the prince had in Andirovia. Suddenly, she remembered her last ride with Kate. "We have haunted woods," she said, triumphantly.

Chapter 5

To Ellie's delight, the prince was at a loss for words. Now it was her turn to tease him. "Don't tell me you don't have any ghosts in Andirovia!" she said.

Prince John looked flustered. "Not that I know of," he admitted, reluctantly. He obviously wasn't used to losing. He thought for a moment and added, "But of course, I don't believe in ghosts, anyway."

At that moment, Kate's grandmother arrived in her best cook's uniform and curtsied to the prince. "I thought you two might be feeling a little hungry," she said, setting a tray of lemonade and cake down on the nearby garden table.

"Thanks," said Ellie. "We were just talking about ghosts."

Kate's grandmother shook her head. "I don't believe in those things," she said. "All that oohing and aahing and frightening people. When I'm dead, I'm sure I'll have better things to do with my time."

As she walked away, John said, "You see. She doesn't believe in them, either. I bet your woods aren't haunted at all."

"Yes, they are," argued Ellie. "There's definitely something there. My friend Kate thinks it's the ghost of someone who grew trees. She calls him Archduke Edgar."

John gulped down a chunk of cake before continuing the argument.

"That's silly," he said. "Archdukes don't do gardening. They lead armies and fight battles and stuff like that."

"Maybe this one didn't," said Ellie.

"You don't get to be a ghost by planting seeds," said John. "Everyone knows you have to die in some interesting way."

Ellie crossed her arms and stared at him. "So, you admit ghosts do exist," she said, unable to keep the tone of superiority out of her voice.

The prince stared back defiantly. "Not yet," he said. "But, tell me more about those woods. Has anything interesting ever happened there?"

"That's what I'm planning to find out," explained Ellie. "Do you want to help?"

Prince John shrugged. "I guess so. Anything's better than croquet."

"We've got lots of history books in our royal library," declared Ellie. "Some of them may mention our woods."

They drank the last of the lemonade and headed for the palace library. It was an enormous room with a high ceiling and shelves stacked with leather-bound books, each stamped with a golden crown.

The prince looked around in dismay. "How are we ever going to find what we want?"

Ellie wasn't exactly sure. She'd been daydreaming about show jumping when Miss Stringle had taught her about library classification. She knew even less about it than she did about spoons. "Perhaps we just start looking," she said, without much enthusiasm.

"I'm not reading all those books," declared Prince John. "It would be much better to look on the Internet. You do have a computer, don't you?"

"Of course I do," Ellie snapped. "It's in my room."

"Let's go, then," said John, as he urged her out of the library. "We can play some computer games, too. They're much better than stupid croquet."

Ellie sighed. She hoped he wouldn't think her room was stupid. As they climbed the stairs, she tried to prepare him for the room's overwhelming pinkness. "It's my father's fault," she explained. "He seems to think all princesses like pink, but *I* don't."

To her surprise, John was sympathetic. "My father's like that, too. He thinks all princes like boats, but I hate them. I get seasick too easily."

His reaction filled Ellie with renewed confidence. If he understood what she went through with her father, he might stop making fun of her. She threw open her bedroom door and waved him in. "The computer's by the window," she said.

Prince John stepped inside and stared around the room in surprise. Then he burst out laughing.

Chapter 6

Ellie glared at John. "I told you it was pink," she said, angrily.

"But you didn't tell me about the ponies," he replied.

Ellie looked around the room and saw what he meant. She had been so worried about the pink that she'd forgotten about everything else. Pony posters covered the pink walls, pony books crammed the pink bookcases, and pony statues stood on every pink surface.

She stared at him defiantly. "Don't you dare make fun of me!" she shouted. "I just like ponies. There's nothing wrong with that."

"I know there's not," said John, with a

huge smile that lit up his normally sour face. "I'm not laughing at you."

"Then what's so funny?" said Ellie. She had calmed down a little, but she was still suspicious.

"Nothing," said John. "I'm just laughing because I'm happy. I've finally met someone who likes ponies as much as I do."

Ellie stared at him in astonishment. "You like them, too?" she asked.

"More than anything in the world," said John. "I'd have told you before, but my father ordered me not to talk about ponies while I'm here. He thought it would bore you as much as it bores him."

Now it was Ellie's turn to laugh. "He was wrong about that. But my dad's just as bad. He said I couldn't ride, or go to the stable, or play with my ponies. I'm supposed to give you all my attention."

John walked across the room and stared thoughtfully out of the window. Then he turned and grinned at Ellie. "I'm supposed to be polite to you. My father was very insistent about that. So, now that you've started talking about ponies, perhaps I'd better join in. It would be very rude if I didn't."

"Yes, it would be," said Ellie with a smile. "And if you want to go to the stable, I guess that I have to go with you. I wouldn't be giving you my full attention if I didn't."

"Then what are we waiting for?" said John, as he headed for the door. Ellie was right behind him.

Although they had convinced themselves that they weren't breaking any rules, they didn't want to take any risks. They checked carefully to make sure no one was looking before they headed for the stable.

Meg was surprised to see them. "I thought you weren't allowed to come here for a few days," she said to Ellie.

After she had reassured Meg that everything was fine, Ellie introduced her to John. Then she took the prince to meet Shadow, Rainbow, Moonbeam, and Sundance, while he told her about the two chestnut mares he had back in Andirovia. Ellie noted that he had fewer ponies than she did, but she didn't feel the need to rub it in. They were friends now, not competitors.

"Can we do anything to help?" Ellie asked Meg.

"I haven't groomed Rainbow and Sundance yet," said Meg. She paused and raised her eyebrows as she looked at their clothes. "But neither of you look dressed for stable work."

"Oh, that doesn't matter," said Ellie. She turned to John and asked, "Do you want to do some grooming?"

"Definitely," said John. Then, he looked embarrassed and added, "But I don't actually know how. The servants always do it for me at home."

Ellie knew exactly how he felt. Not long ago, she had been just like him. She had never been allowed to look after her ponies until Meg came along. "Don't worry," she said. "I'll show you what to do."

She grabbed the brush kit from the tack room and tied the two ponies up outdoors in the sunshine. Then she showed John how to use the different brushes and the hoof pick. It felt good to be the knowledgeable one of the pair. There was no way he could think she was stupid anymore.

Half an hour later, they stepped back and admired the results of their work with satisfaction. Both ponies were spotlessly clean. Their coats gleamed, their tails hung straight and untangled, and their hooves shone with hoof oil.

"I'd love to go for a ride on this one," said John, as he stroked Sundance's nose. The chestnut pony whickered with pleasure. Then Sundance rubbed the side of his head on the prince's shoulder so hard that he nearly knocked him over.

Ellie grinned. "Well, if you want to ride, it's obviously my duty to go with you." She paused and looked down at her skirt. "I'll have to get changed first. Do you need to borrow some clothes? I'm afraid everything's pink, even my spare helmet."

"I don't care," said John. "I'll wear anything if it means I can ride."

"Let's go, then," said Ellie. "The sooner we change, the sooner we can get back."

They were in such a hurry that they forgot to check to see if anyone was around. They raced out of the stable and bumped right into the Emperor of Andirovia.

Chapter 7

To Ellie's horror, the Emperor was not alone. The King was beside him, the Queen and the Empress close behind. All four of them stared at Ellie and John in dismay.

"You are filthy!" yelled the Emperor, pointing at John in disgust.

"So are you, Aurelia," added the Queen.

Ellie looked down at herself and saw that they were right. Her hands were caked with dirt, her legs and skirt were dusty, and her blouse was no longer white. John looked even worse. He had spilled hoof oil down his trousers and in his attempts to wipe it off had gotten it on his hands and finally wiped it on his nose.

The Empress walked up to John and sniffed suspiciously. "You smell like a horse," she said in an accusing voice.

"What have you been doing, Aurelia?" the King said sternly. "I distinctly told you not to go to the stable."

Ellie bit her lip nervously as she looked at their angry faces. If she couldn't talk her way out of this, she was in big trouble. "But John wanted to see the ponies, and you told me to entertain him."

"Ponies, ponies, ponies," shouted the Emperor. He glowered at John in frustration. "I told you not to talk about them while we were here."

John put on a suitably apologetic face. "Princess Aurelia started talking about them first," he said in a very polite voice. "I thought it would have been rude not to reply."

The Emperor turned to the King in surprise. "Is your child as pony-crazed as mine is?" he asked.

The King sighed. "She's got to be even crazier," he said. "It's so hard to live with."

The two rulers started commiserating with each other on the problems of parenthood. They seemed to have completely lost interest in their children.

Ellie walked over to her mother. "Can we go now?" she whispered. "We want to go for a ride."

"You can go and get clean," said the Queen, firmly. "You are both having lunch with us, and after that the prime minister has promised to entertain John with some of his magic tricks."

"But what about our ride?" asked Ellie. Magic tricks didn't sound as fun as riding ponies.

John looked at his mother with big, round eyes. Please, Mom," he said.

Ellie was impressed. She wished she could put on such an innocent expression whenever she wanted. It would have been really useful when she was in trouble.

John's approach obviously worked. The Empress smiled. "Maybe they could go later," she suggested to the Queen. After looking at their watches several times, the two mothers agreed that riding at four was a reasonable idea.

"That's so far away," groaned John as he walked back to the palace with Ellie.

"But going later means Kate can come with us," said Ellie. "We can go right up to the top of the hill and show you the view."

"I've got a much better idea," said John. "Let's go to the haunted woods and try to find the ghost."

Ellie's eyes lit up with excitement. Was there a chance that together they could really solve the mystery of the ghost?

Ellie got ready as quickly as she could. She had just finished dressing when John knocked on her bedroom door.

"There's just time to do some Internet ghost hunting before lunch," he said, as he walked over to the computer.

He was right. There were dozens of useful Web sites, and they soon had a list of everything they needed in order to track down a ghost.

"We'd better take halters, too," said Ellie. "We might need to tie the ponies up."

"That's a good idea," said John. "I can bring my camera, watch, and tape recorder. Can you find everything else?"

Ellie nodded as she looked down at the piece of paper in her hand. It was a funny list. She might have thought of backpacks and notebooks by herself, but she would never have dreamed of taking talcum powder, a thermometer, and a set of wind chimes.

Hunting ghosts was more complicated than she'd expected. What would they do if they actually found one?

Chapter 8

Lunch that day was more elaborate than usual. A whole roasted goose sat on a side table. Ellie eyed it warily and chose to eat cheese instead. She liked geese and would rather have seen them swimming.

The meal dragged on and on, and so did the magic display that followed it. The prime minister was not a very good magician. Ellie could see how he did many of his tricks, but

she pretended that she couldn't. She gasped with amazement when he produced an egg from behind her ear. She clapped loudly when he turned a bottle into a bunch of flowers, and she pretended not to notice that the rabbit in his act had chewed a hole in the prime minister's top hat and escaped.

The hands of the ornate gold

clock on the mantelpiece moved frustratingly slowly. Ellie felt as if the show's performance would go on forever. But just before three-thirty, the final trick was done, and Ellie and John were free to leave. There was just enough time to gather up all the ghost-hunting equipment and get changed before their ride.

Kate was waiting for them in the stable when they arrived. She was holding the message they had sent her and was looking very excited. Ellie quickly introduced Kate and John to each other. "I brought these, just in case," Kate said, holding out three cloves of garlic.

"In case of what?" asked John. "Garlic's for keeping vampires away, not ghosts."

Kate thrust the garlic back in her pocket.

"I'll take them, anyway. They might come in handy for something."

Ellie showed John how to put the saddle and bridle on Sundance while Kate got Rainbow and Moonbeam ready. Then they stuffed the ponies' halters in their backpacks, mounted the ponies, and headed out on their ride.

Rainbow was frisky. She tossed her head and kept trying to trot. Ellie had to keep a firm hold on the reins to keep her at a walk. She wanted to give John time to get used to Sundance before they tried going any faster.

She didn't have to worry. The chestnut pony was as well behaved as ever, and John was a good rider.

They turned in to a field. Rainbow started to trot as soon as she felt the grass under her feet. Ellie struggled to make the gray pony walk rather than trot, but a sudden commotion drew her attention away from Rainbow for a moment. Moonbeam was so excited to be out in the field that she'd lifted her back legs off the ground in a huge bucking movement.

"Eeek!" cried Kate as she fought to stay in the saddle. "These ponies just have way too much energy."

"Let's use some of it up," said Ellie. She glanced over at John. "Are you ready to go faster?"

John grinned. "I'm ready when you are."

Ellie stopped trying to restrain Rainbow. Kate and John followed Ellie's lead around the edge of the field.

When they reached the top of the hill, they slowed to a walk in order to pass through a gate, on to a stretch of wide-open land. It was the perfect place to let the ponies gallop.

Ellie squeezed slightly with her legs, and Rainbow leaped forward eagerly. Soon she was racing side by side with Sundance and Moonbeam as they galloped across the grass.

Ellie leaned forward, urging Rainbow on. It was wonderful to be riding again. She would have happily galloped forever. But eventually Rainbow started to get tired. Ellie let her slow to a canter, then a trot, and finally to a walk.

The galloping had used up the ponies' extra energy. Now they were all better behaved. Rainbow seemed content to walk, so Ellie lengthened the reins to let the pony stretch her neck and relax.

They rode farther and farther from the palace until they found the gate Ellie and Kate had passed through the other day. They walked through it and along the edge of the cornfield, then turned right when they reached the high wall near the woods. Ellie felt a shiver of excitement when she saw the haunted woods in front of them.

She stopped Rainbow. The path ahead looked even darker and more mysterious than it had the first time. Ellie looked at

John. "This was your idea," she said. "So . . . what do we do now?"

"We'd better get organized," he replied. He switched on the tape recorder in his pocket, clipped a microphone to the collar of his shirt, and said in a serious voice, "Time: four forty-six P.M. Temperature?" He looked questioningly at Kate.

She stared back at him. "The thermometer's in my backpack. I can't use it while I'm riding."

John shrugged and started again. "Time: four forty-seven P.M. Temperature: very hot. We are just entering the haunted woods."

Ellie made Rainbow walk forward. The gray pony snorted suspiciously as she stepped into the dark tunnel made by the overhanging branches. Her ears were pricked forward, alert to possible danger.

They moved forward quietly. The ponies' hooves made almost no sound on the layer of dead leaves covering the ground. Ellie glanced nervously from side to side, expecting something to jump out at her at any moment.

Suddenly, the silence was broken by John. "Time: five oh-two. We are now inside the woods. The temperature is noticeably lower."

Ellie shivered. He was right. It was chilly. Was that because the trees blocked the sun, or was there some other reason? Was there a ghost making the air so cold?

Chapter 9

The path led them deeper and deeper into the woods. Suddenly, Ellie realized that they were almost at the place where Rainbow had spooked on their last ride. She leaned forward and gave the pony a reassuring pat. "There's nothing to be scared of," she said, as confidently as she could. But she kept a firm hold on the reins just in case.

Rainbow walked forward steadily, each

step bringing her closer to the frightening spot. Ellie started to relax. “Maybe the ghost isn’t here today,” she said.

She had spoken too soon. Rainbow suddenly stopped dead and then whirled to the right. “Steady, girl,” said Ellie, as she stopped the pony and turned her to face forward again. “There’s nothing there.” She pushed the pony on with her legs and felt her take a step forward.

Just when Ellie thought the trouble was over, Rainbow changed direction in mid-step and spun again, this time to the left. Ellie was caught off balance. She lost both stirrups and slid sideways in the saddle.

“Steady,” she called out again, but it was no use—the pony was too frightened to listen; she whirled once more, and Ellie slipped over the pony's shoulder.

"Ouch!" Ellie cried as she landed in a patch of thorny bushes. She was still holding on tightly to the reins.

"Time: five-fourteen," said John into his tape recorder. "Rainbow has seen something. Is it the ghost?"

Kate jumped down from Moonbeam's back and helped free Ellie from the prickly bushcs.

Ellie gently stroked Rainbow. "It's all right," she whispered in a soothing voice. "You don't have to go any farther." Then she turned to the others. "We'll have to hunt on foot now," she announced. "It's not fair to make her go on when she's so frightened."

"Let's tie the ponies up here," said John.

"No," said Ellie. "They should be farther away, so they won't be scared." She led Rainbow back along the path until the gray pony seemed more relaxed. "This is good," she said as she tied Rainbow to a tree with the halter and lead rope from her backpack. "Rainbow should be okay here."

Kate and John joined her and pulled halters from their backpacks. Soon, all three ponies were tied up side by side. Sundance immediately started to doze. Rainbow and

Moonbeam looked calmer now.

When the ponies were taken care of, John took charge. "I'll take the camera," he said. "You take the wind chimes, Kate. Hang it over there in that tree."

"Why?" asked Kate, who hadn't seen any of the Web sites and didn't know about the ghost-hunting plan.

"It's to spot movement in the air," explained John. Then he handed Ellie the talcum powder. "I want you to sprinkle that all over the ground. It'll help reveal any ghostly footprints."

Ellie walked nervously along the path, glancing from side to side and ready to run at any moment. When she was sure she was past whatever it was that Rainbow had seen, she stopped and walked backward toward

John, sprinkling powder on the path as she went.

Halfway along she was joined by Kate, who had just finished tying up the wind chimes.

"Do you want this?" said Kate, as she pressed something into Ellie's spare hand. Her voice was edged with fear.

Ellie stopped sprinkling the powder for a moment and looked down to see what Kate was holding. It was the garlic.

"I know John said it wouldn't help, but he might be wrong," Kate whispered.

"Thanks," said Ellie. She clutched the garlic tightly. The feel of it was comforting.

"Time: five forty-one," said John into his tape recorder. "Everything is prepared. We are now waiting for something to happen."

"Let's wait over there," said Ellie, pointing at a fallen log close to the path.

The others agreed, but, on the way, John stopped dramatically and pointed at the ground.

"Time: five forty-four," he said. "We see a footprint in the powder."

Ellie's heart skipped a beat as she stared at the path. John was right. There was a footprint. Was it the ghost's?

John pulled out a magnifying glass and

stared through it at the footprint. “Mmm,” he said. “It’s not very big. Maybe it’s the ghost of a child.” He paused again and added, “A child wearing boots.”

Kate coughed and looked embarrassed. “I think it might be me,” she said. She stepped forward and put her foot gently into the print. It was a perfect match. “I’m so sorry. I thought I’d managed not to step in the powder.”

“Time: five forty-eight,” said John. “A false alarm.”

Ellie breathed a sigh of relief. Although the idea of hunting ghosts had sounded like fun, she wasn’t sure she actually wanted to find one. She sat down on the log hoping that nothing else would happen.

For a few minutes, nothing did. They sat

waiting. Suddenly, a tinkling sound broke the silence. It was the sound of the wind chimes. But there wasn't any wind.

Ellie gulped and looked at Kate, who in turn looked at John, who looked right back at Ellie. Then they all looked in the direction of the noise, each thinking the same thing: was there really a ghost in the woods?

Chapter 10

"What was that?" cried Ellie as she jumped to her feet. She tightened her grip on the garlic, just in case.

"Maybes it's the ghost," said John. For the first time, there was a trace of fear in his voice. He seemed to have forgotten about the tape recorder.

The wind chimes tinkled again. This time Ellie was looking at them. She saw the leaves above them move as well. "There's something in the tree," she said.

"Is it the ghost?" whispered Kate in a frightened voice. She ducked down behind the log as if it would protect her.

The leaves moved again, and Ellie saw a flash of chestnut fur among them. A red squirrel bounded into sight. It sat on the branch for a moment before scampering up the trunk of the tree and disappearing from view.

"Phew," said Ellie in relief. "I've never been so happy to see a squirrel."

"Neither have I," said

Kate. She stood up, brushing leaves and dirt from her jodhpurs.

John took a deep breath. He looked confused. "Do you smell something?" he asked.

Ellie sniffed the air. There definitely was a smell, but she couldn't figure out what it was. "Where's it coming from?" she asked.

The three of them spread out as they tried to sniff out the source. The smell faded when they walked back toward the ponies. It was also weaker when they went farther along the path, and when they turned right and walked among the trees. It grew stronger only when they walked near the wall.

"There must be something behind there," said Ellie, pointing at the bricks.

"It's not the ghost, is it?" asked Kate nervously. "Ghosts don't smell, do they?"

"Some of them do," said John. "Lots of haunted places have strange smells."

"And so do lots of nonhaunted ones," said Ellie, to reassure herself as much as Kate.

The only way to find out if it was the ghost was to look on the other side of the wall. But it was too high and hard to climb.

"Look over there!" shouted John, pointing to a nearby tree. "If we climb on those branches, we should be able to swing over onto the top of the wall."

Ellie looked up at the branches in dismay. She had never climbed a tree before and wasn't sure how to start.

Kate seemed to know what Ellie was thinking. "It's not hard," she said. "You just grab hold of this branch, put one foot on this branch and then the other on that one." As she spoke, she moved up the tree like a monkey. She made climbing look easy.

For Ellie, it wasn't. She had to try three times before she managed to grab a branch.

Then her feet slipped on the bark as she tried to heave herself up onto the trunk. She managed to make it only because John gave her a shove from underneath. Then he followed her.

Kate was waiting for them impatiently. "The next part should be even easier," she said. "I found three strong branches that reach the wall. We can each take one and wiggle along them."

Ellie looked at the branches and at the ground beneath them. It was a long way to fall. For a brief moment, she wondered if she should stay where she was and let the others go on without her. Then her curiosity overcame her fear. She wanted to see for herself what was hiding on the other side of that wall.

She wiggled onto the middle branch and, trying hard not to look down, started to edge her way along. Kate and John made their way along the other two branches, and they all reached the wall at the same time.

Together they peered down—straight into a pair of eyes. Something was looking up at them. But it wasn't a ghost. It was an enormous pig.

Kate pointed at it in delight. "That

explains the smell," she said.

"But it doesn't explain the ghost," said John.

"Yes, it does," laughed Ellie. "It says in one of my books that lots of ponies are frightened of pigs. Rainbow must be one of them. She didn't see a ghost at all. She smelled the pig."

"So there's no ghostly gardener," said Kate.

"And no haunted woods," said John.

Neither of them sounded very disappointed. Ellie suspected they were as relieved as she was. The ghost hunt had been quite scary enough without finding a real ghost.

"But there is an Archduke Edgar," said John. He stood at attention on top of the wall and saluted the pig. "I bring you greetings from Andirovia, Your Royal Highness," he said with a big grin.

Ellie and her friends collapsed with laughter.

Here's a sneak peek at the next adventure of the

Pony-Crazed Princess

in

Princess Ellie's Starlight Adventure

Princess Ellie's Starlight Adventure

Chapter 1

"Princess Aurelia!" The shout echoed down the palace corridor.

Princess Ellie groaned. She was on her way to the stable and didn't want to stop. She didn't like to be called by her real name, either. She liked "Ellie" much more.

The owner of the voice came rushing toward the princess. It was a palace maid, who looked very flustered and out of breath.

"You'd better come quickly, Your Highness. The King and Queen are very angry."

Ellie followed the maid back along the corridor, wondering what she'd done wrong this time. For once, she couldn't think of anything. She had been very polite for the last few days, and it had been a long time since she'd shown up for dinner in her jodhpurs or muddy boots.

The King and Queen were waiting impatiently for her in their favorite part of the royal garden. Their arms were crossed, and their faces looked even angrier than Ellie had expected.

"Look at the mess you've made, Aurelia," roared the King, as he pointed at the grass. The normally smooth green surface of the lawn was covered with hoofprints.

"How dare you ride in my garden?" wailed the Queen. She sniffed angrily and dabbed away a tear using a handkerchief embroidered with silver crowns.

"It wasn't me," said Ellie.

"Don't tell lies," snapped the King.

Ellie resisted the temptation to snap back. She knew from experience that that would only make matters worse. "I am telling the truth," she insisted, as calmly as possible. "I've got all of the palace grounds to ride in. I don't need to use the royal garden."

"Hmmm," said the Queen thoughtfully. "Aurelia does have a point, my dear."

The King was less convinced. He stared suspiciously at Ellie and asked, "How do you explain the hoofprints, then?"

Ellie bent down and ran her fingers

around one of the holes in the grass as she tried to think of an explanation. Meg, the royal groom, had a horse of her own, but she was too smart to ride Gypsy in the garden. Ellie's four ponies were the only other suspects.

"If you haven't ridden here, who has?" asked the Queen, when Ellie didn't answer. "It certainly wasn't Kate."

Ellie didn't need reminding. She had been lonely ever since her best friend had gone to visit her parents, who were working in a distant desert. Life was much more exciting and fun when Kate stayed with her grandmother, the palace cook. The two girls spent all their time together, riding Ellie's ponies or helping out at the stable. Once, they had even saved Sundance's life, after he somehow managed to get out of his stall in a storm.

That memory gave Ellie an idea. "One of the ponies must have escaped," she announced.

"That's a possibility," admitted the Queen. "But that doesn't mean we can have ponies running all over the place doing whatever they please."

"Definitely not," said the King, firmly. "Tell Meg to make sure it doesn't happen again."

Ellie promised that she would. Then she ran to the stable to check on her ponies. To her surprise, none of them was missing. Moonbeam, Rainbow, Sundance, and Shadow were all in their stalls, happily munching hay. So was Gypsy.

"That's really strange," said Meg, when she heard what had happened.

"Maybe one of them escaped and then came back," suggested Ellie. "Sundance knows how to undo locks."

"He must have learned how to redo them, too," replied Meg. "His door was definitely closed tight this morning." She looked at Ellie's anxious face and smiled. "Don't worry. I'll double-check everything tonight before I go to bed, and I'll put a special clip on Sundance's door, so he can't undo it and get out."

"That should stop it from happening again," said Ellie, confidently. If there was no way her ponies could escape, there was no way they could do any damage. By the next morning, her parents would probably have forgotten all about the mysterious hoof-prints.

Unfortunately, Ellie was wrong. Before she'd even had time for breakfast, she was summoned to the garden again, and so was Meg. Ellie's parents were even angrier than before. The King's face was nearly as red as the ruby in his crown.

"Look at this. There are even more hoof-prints than yesterday," said the King, as he stared accusingly at both of the girls.

"And my prize petunias are ruined," added the Queen, holding up the mangled plants. "Your ponies have been eating my flowers."

"But they couldn't have been," said Ellie.

"They must have been," snapped the King.

"Excuse me, Your Majesties," said Meg, politely. "The ponies were all shut securely in their stalls when I went to bed last night, and they were still there this morning."

"Then they must have been out in between," said the Queen. "It's the only possible explanation. They are the only ponies at the palace."

The King glared at Meg. "This is your fault. Go back to the stable, and make sure this doesn't happen again. If it does, we may have to reconsider your position."

To find out what happens next, read

Princess Ellie's Starlight Adventure